A Day
in the
Salt Marsh

By Kevin Kurtz
Illustrations by Consie Powell

To my parents-Thanks for eighteen years of free food and shelter—KK

For Annie, whose friendship makes me rich—CP

Thanks to Susan-Marie Stedman, Wetland Team Leader at NOAA
Fisheries Office of Habitat Conservation for verifying the accuracy of the
book, including the "For Creative Minds" educational section.

Publisher's Cataloging-In-Publication Data
Kurtz, Kevin.
A day in the salt marsh / by Kevin Kurtz ; illustrations by Consie Powell.
p. : col. ill. ; cm.
Summary: Rhyming verse introduces readers to hourly changes in the
salt marsh as the tide comes and goes.
Includes "For Creative Minds" section.
Interest age level: 004-008.
Interest grade level: P-3.
ISBN: 978-0-9768823-5-0 (hardcover)
ISBN: 978-1-934359-19-8 (pbk.)

1. Salt marshes--Juvenile literature. 2. Salt marsh ecology--Juvenile literature. 3. Salt marsh animals--Juvenile literature.
4. Salt marshes. 5. Salt marsh ecology. 6. Salt marsh animals. 7. Stories in rhyme. I. Powell, Consie. II. Title.

QH541.5.S24 K87 2007
577.69   2006940903

Printed in China

Sylvan Dell Publishing
976 Houston Northcutt Blvd., Suite 3
Mt. Pleasant, SC 29464

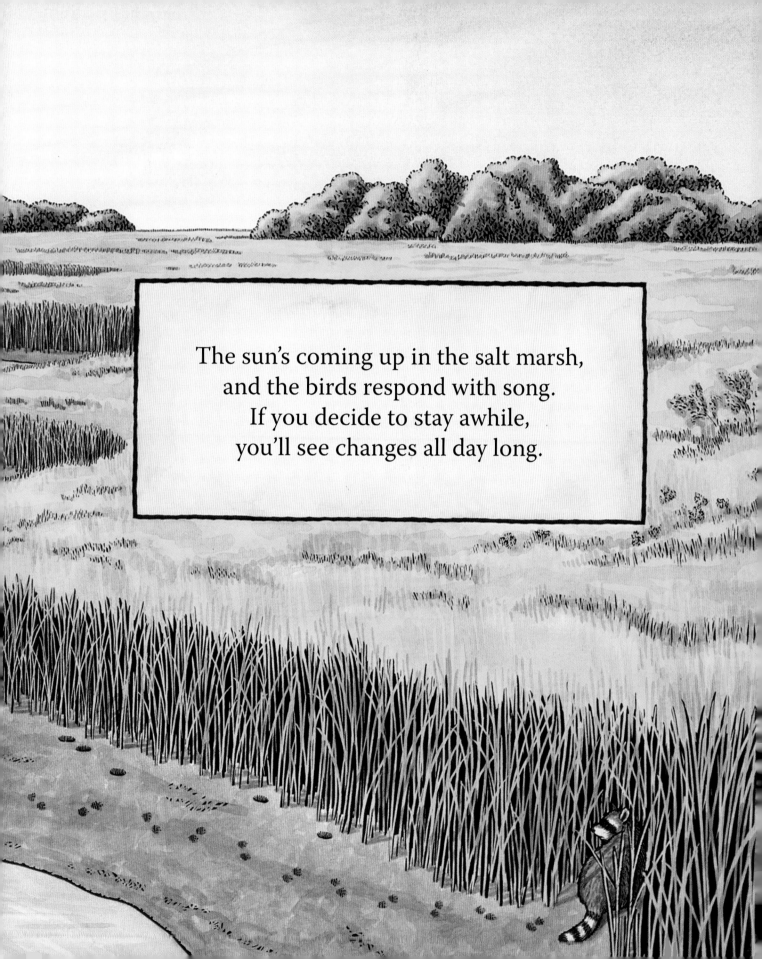

The sun's coming up in the salt marsh,
and the birds respond with song.
If you decide to stay awhile,
you'll see changes all day long.

It's eight o'clock in the salt marsh;
the tide is really low.
The fiddler crabs upon the mud
are putting on a show.

They wave their claws to the left,
then wave them to the right,
and if a rival gets too close,
the crabs will start to fight.

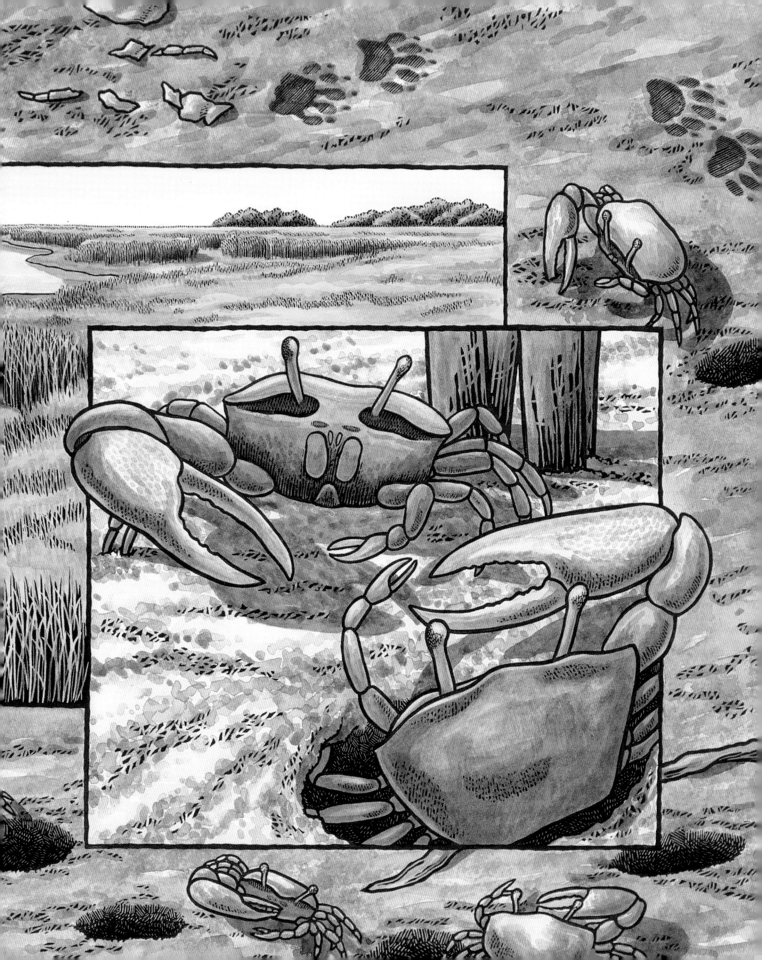

It's nine o'clock in the salt marsh;
the tide is coming back.
And on the muddy bank,
you'll hear a quiet "crack!"

A terrapin is eating
while resting on the ground.
It bites into a snail's shell
and makes a popping sound.

It's ten o'clock in the salt marsh;
the tide's now in the grass.
The tiny periwinkle snails
wait for the tide to pass.

Clinging to the blades of grass,
they climb without a sound
staying above the rising water
to avoid being drowned.

It's eleven o'clock in the salt marsh;
the tide is getting high.
Over in the tidal creek,
a blue crab skitters by.

The blue crab isn't picky
and will eat 'most any dish.
It even eats sea cucumber
or a stinky piece of fish.

It's twelve o'clock in the salt marsh;
the tide is rising fast.
A grey fin breaks the water
as a dolphin swims right past!

Look! It's moving quickly—
just like it's in a race.
The small fish swim before it
as the dolphin gives them chase.

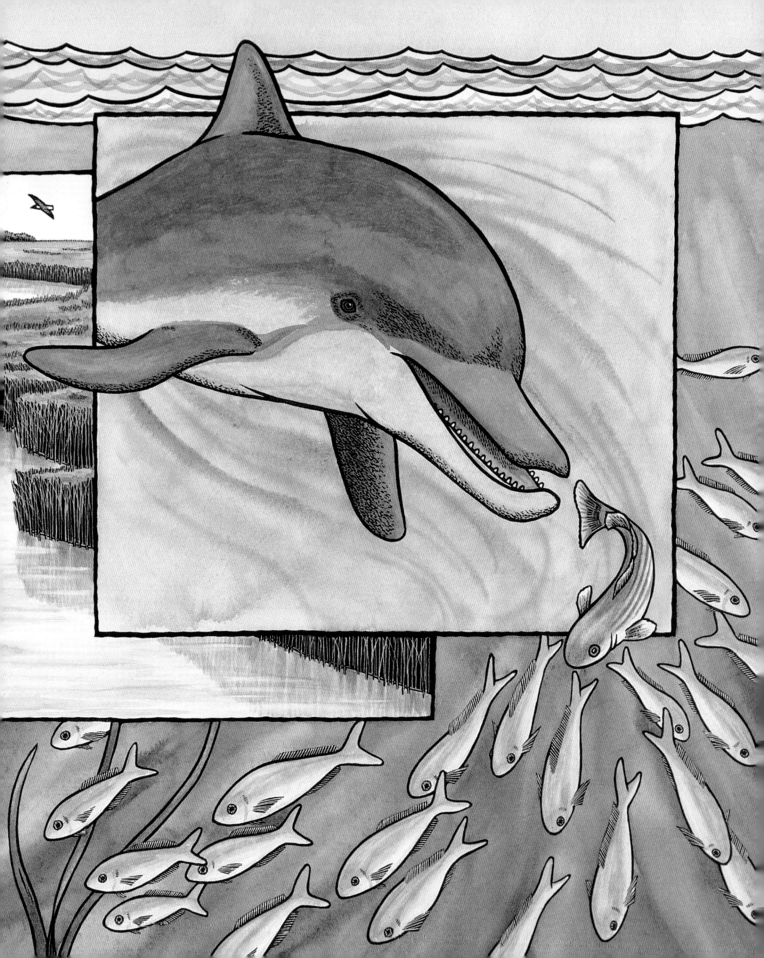

It's one o'clock in the salt marsh;
the tide is very high.
The grass is under water,
and yet it doesn't die.

The cordgrass drinks saltwater
as the wind blows it about.
The leaves hold in the water,
but spit the salt back out.

It's two o'clock in the salt marsh.
A fish, small and tiny
swimming all around the grass
with scales so small and shiny.

The marsh is like a nursery
where little fish can hide.
They eat the food that's brought their way
with each new rising tide.

It's three o'clock in the salt marsh,
and on and off all day
running, splashing, swimming
the river otters play.

Two pups begin to wrestle,
a game of one-on-one.
At first their mother watches,
then joins them in the fun.

It's four o'clock in the salt marsh,
and over by the tidal creek
stands a grey and stately bird
with a long, pointy beak.

The great blue heron waits quietly,
but when it sees its prey,
its beak hits the water
and the fish can't get away.

It's five o'clock in the salt marsh,
and the water's going down.
Over on the muddy bank
a horseshoe crab's aground.

It doesn't seem to move at all
yet if you look and smell,
it's not the live horseshoe crab
but just the molted shell!

It's six o'clock in the salt marsh;
the oysters no longer hide.
They're out in the sunlight,
uncovered by the tide.

Oysters hold up the banks
so the grass can grow.
Grass supports the food web,
in the daily salt marsh show.

The sun's going down in the salt marsh;
the day is almost through.
But if you're back tomorrow,
you'll see other changes too!

For Creative Minds

Salt Marsh Plants and Animals

Read the descriptions of the Salt Marsh animals and match each to the appropriate picture.

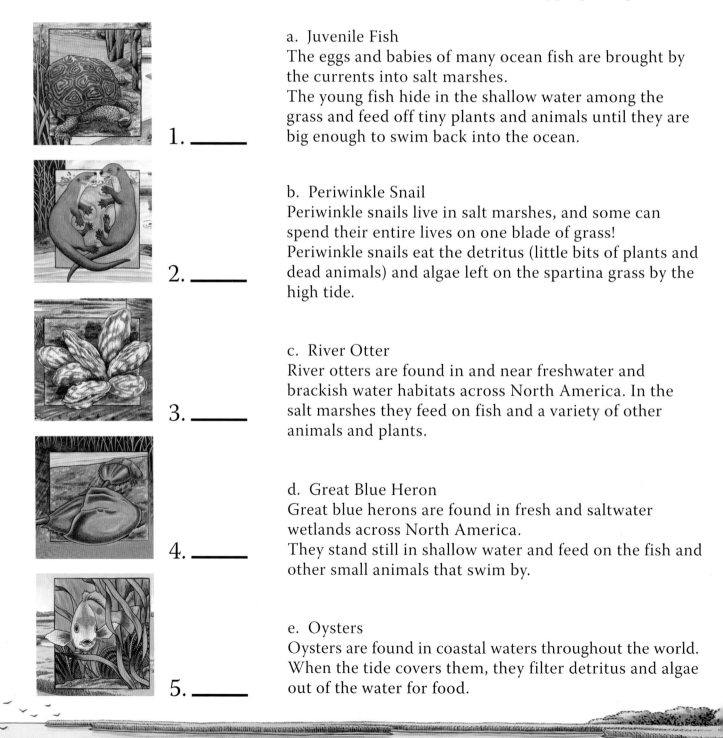

1. _____

a. Juvenile Fish
The eggs and babies of many ocean fish are brought by the currents into salt marshes.
The young fish hide in the shallow water among the grass and feed off tiny plants and animals until they are big enough to swim back into the ocean.

2. _____

b. Periwinkle Snail
Periwinkle snails live in salt marshes, and some can spend their entire lives on one blade of grass!
Periwinkle snails eat the detritus (little bits of plants and dead animals) and algae left on the spartina grass by the high tide.

3. _____

c. River Otter
River otters are found in and near freshwater and brackish water habitats across North America. In the salt marshes they feed on fish and a variety of other animals and plants.

4. _____

d. Great Blue Heron
Great blue herons are found in fresh and saltwater wetlands across North America.
They stand still in shallow water and feed on the fish and other small animals that swim by.

5. _____

e. Oysters
Oysters are found in coastal waters throughout the world. When the tide covers them, they filter detritus and algae out of the water for food.

f. Blue Crab
In the United States blue crabs are found in the coastal
waters of the Atlantic Ocean and Gulf of Mexico.
They are scavengers and eat dead animals.

_____ 6.

g. Bottlenose Dolphin
With the exception of the Arctic and Antarctic,
bottlenose dolphins are found in coastal and ocean
waters all around the world.
They often work together to feed on small fish and
squid. In the southeastern United States, they have even
been seen in salt marshes knocking fish out of the water
and eating them on the land!

_____ 7.

h. Diamondback Terrapin
Diamondback terrapins are the only turtles that live in
salt marshes.
They feed on crabs, snails, insects, fish and sometimes
worms and aquatic plants.

_____ 8.

i. Fiddler Crab
Fiddler crabs live in the mud in salt marshes and tidal flats.
Fiddler crabs scoop up mouthfuls of dirt and separate
the algae (their food) from the sand that they spit back
out.

_____ 9.

j. Horseshoe Crab
Horseshoe crabs are found in coastal waters of the
Atlantic and Gulf of Mexico. They live on the tidal flats
and at the bottom of tidal creeks.
They look through the sand and mud for shrimp, worms,
and other small animals.

_____ 10.

Tidal Animals Activity

Salt marshes are wetlands found in areas where rivers meet the oceans (bays and estuaries). The daily rising (flood) and falling (ebb) saltwater tides make this one of the most difficult habitats for plants and animals to survive. *Look at the animals below. Which of the animals are most likely to be in the salt marsh at low tide (when there's not much salt water), and which animals are most likely to be in the marsh at high tide (when there's lots of salt water)?*

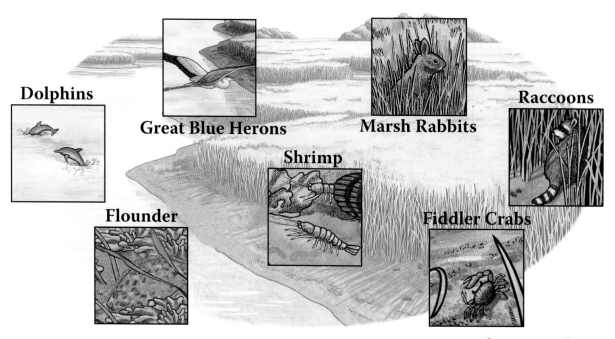

Dolphins

Great Blue Herons

Marsh Rabbits

Raccoons

Shrimp

Flounder

Fiddler Crabs

Answers:
Low tide: raccoons, marsh rabbits, fiddler crabs, and great blue herons
High tide: dolphins, shrimp, and flounder.

What Causes Tides?

As the moon revolves around the earth, gravity pulls the ocean water on the near side of the earth towards it, making a bulge. Because of centrifugal force (like water in a spinning bucket), the water on the opposite side of the earth makes another bulge. These bulges draw water from other parts of the oceans creating two dips. These bulges and dips eventually reach land as high and low tides.

Tides are not the same everywhere on the earth and they change daily. A high tide one day will arrive approximately 50 minutes after it did the day before. Most areas have two tide cycles a day, but there are some areas that only have one. The difference between high tide and low tide is usually a few feet, but it can vary from just a few inches to well over 40 feet in Canada's Bay of Fundy!

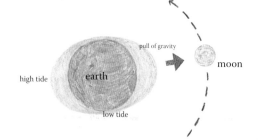

Why are Salt Marshes Important?

Marshes are one of the most important habitats on the planet! So much grass grows there that the only habitats on earth that produce more plant material per acre than marshes are rainforests!

This grass is very important for life in the ocean. When it dies, the tide carries it into the ocean where its nutrients support a variety of food chains. Many ocean animals would not be able to survive without the marsh grass food for them or the animals they eat.

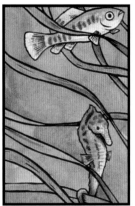

Salt marshes are also safe nursery grounds for many young sea animals. The plants and grass provide food and a place to hide from predators (bigger animals that want to eat them). Almost all animals that we eat as seafood (shrimp, grouper, and flounder) depend on the salt marsh for their babies to grow. Without the salt marsh providing a safe nursery, we wouldn't have seafood to eat.

The salt marsh grasses slow down waves, which helps control floods during hurricanes and other storms.

Salt marsh mud soaks up chemicals in the water and the marsh grass catches litter. This helps the ocean to be cleaner because not as much pollution reaches it.

Salt marshes are not only important to fish and crabs; they are also important to birds. Many migrating birds depend on salt marshes as a resting area and a place to eat while on their long journey.

Spartina and its Adaptations

If you poured salt water on the plants in your yard, they would all die (so don't actually try it). Spartina grass is covered by salt water every day, but it has special glands to get rid of the salt while keeping in the water. *If you lick a spartina blade, you can taste the salt it has spit out!*

Spartina grass has strong, deep roots to hold it firmly in the ground during heavy winds and tide changes. The grass blades are also long and narrow to bend easily during high winds.

There are two types of spartina: the tall spartina is closest to the water and can be over nine feet tall and the short spartina grows to between two and three feet in the meadows or the flats.

Just like other plants, spartina turns green and grows tall in the spring and summer. When fall arrives, it turns brown and starts to break apart. Some of it stays in the marsh where it is eaten by the animals and it helps to fertilize the grass for the next year. Other broken pieces form "wrack," a floating pile of grass that can be carried out to sea or can wash ashore on a beach. Wrack is an important food source and a safe place for tiny little animals.

A type of Spartina called "alterniflora" is native to the East and Gulf Coasts of the United States where it is very important. However, it has somehow found its way to the West Coast of the United States where it has become a serious weed problem. It is growing too fast and taking away habitat from marsh plants (including Spartina foliosa) that are native to that area. *How or why can one plant be really good in one place and bad in another? How do you think plants and animals move from their native area to "invade" a foreign area?*